This book belongs to

Viija Veji

Dedicated to my
mother Isabelle
and to the memory of
my father Edmond,
with deepest heartfelt love.

-Paul M. Crepeau
June 2004

Big Ben and the Small World

by Paul M. Crepeau

Illustrations
by Bryan R. Watai

booksurge.com
booksurgedirect.com

ISBN 1*59457*482*0

Where the creek runs past the railroad track,
Ben lived in a big old shack.

Whenever Ben walked into town,
The word would quickly get around.

He was so big, the legend goes,...

...Buildings shook when he blew his nose.

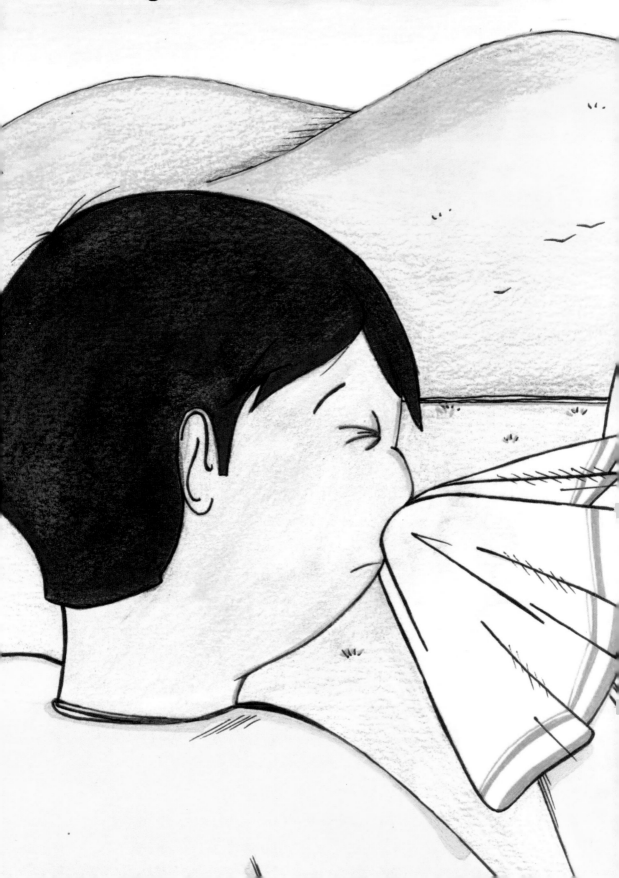

Whenever he let out a sneeze,...

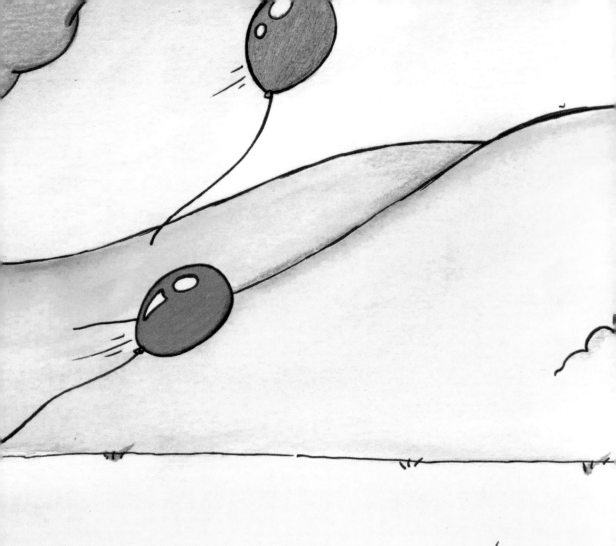

...People would hold on to trees.

They'd yell, "Look out! Here comes
Big Ben!"
No one wanted to be his friend.

In restaurants and public places,
Grownups glared and children
made faces.

On doorways and ceilings Ben bumped his head.

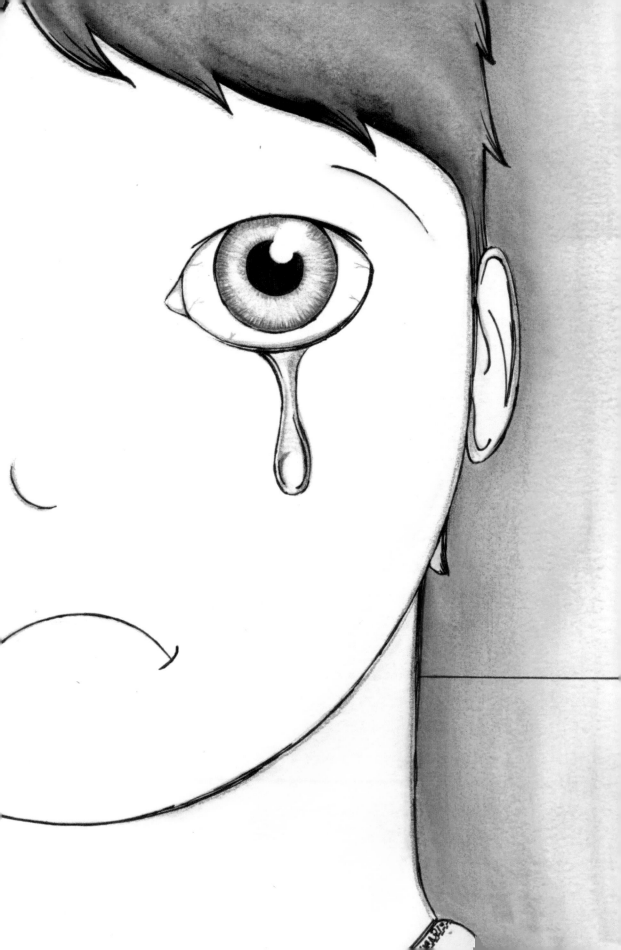

This made Ben so sad, he'd cry;
He'd walk away and wonder, "Why?...

"Why won't they let me be their friend?"
How would you feel if you were Ben?

One quiet day, before anyone knew it,
In the third-floor apartment of
Mary Anne Pruitt,

A fire broke out while she was away.
Just how it started, no one could say.

By the time the fire engine got there,
People had gathered from everywhere.

"Snowball and her kittens are still inside!"
Poor little Mary Anne Pruitt cried.

**Then suddenly, through the smoke
    and heat,
On the third window-ledge above
    the street,**

Five times Snowball went back inside,
Until five kittens were at her side.

But as the firemen fought and
    fought the fire,
The flames grew higher and higher
    and higher.

What else could the firemen do?
They needed a miracle or two.

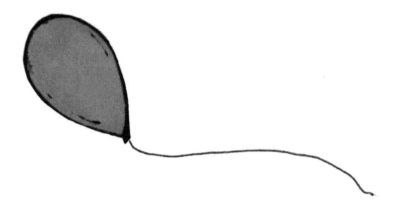

Then someone shouted,
 "Here comes Big Ben!"
Were they overjoyed to see him again!

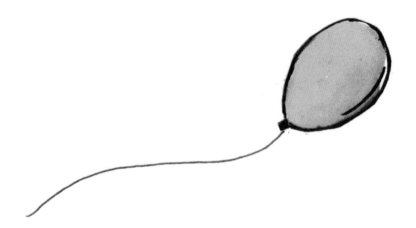

He'd heard the siren and
smelled the smoke,...

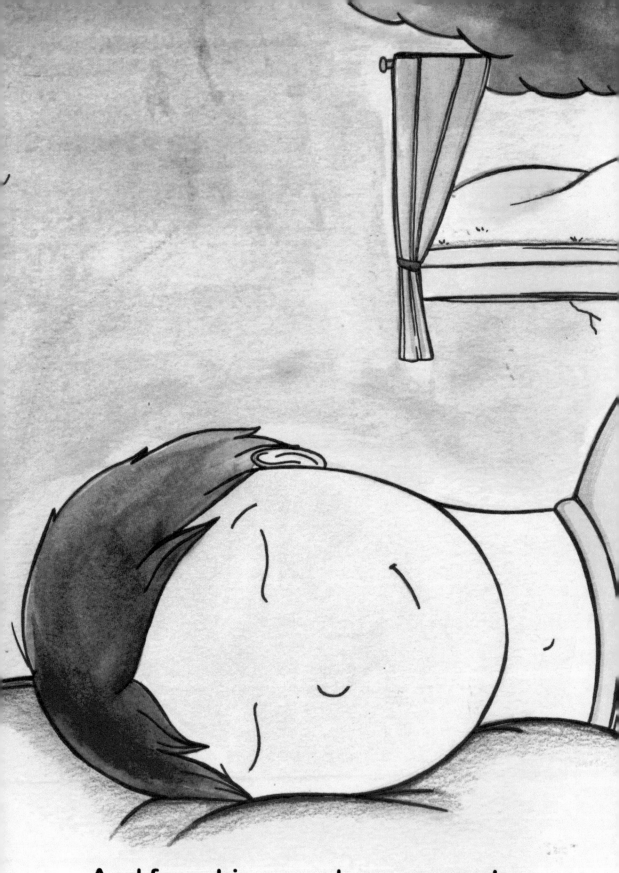

...And from his noonday nap awoke.

His long arms
outstretched,
Ben wasted no time,

And into each hand
a kitten did climb.

Then he placed them gently on
    the ground;
Soon mother and kittens were
    safe and sound.

I was watching T.V. that evening, when
On the seven o' clock news I saw
Big Ben!

He was a hero, it was true!
He'd done what only heroes do.

News of the rescue spread far and wide.
No longer could it be denied:

Ben was a hero, not a clown.
From then on no one put him down.

Now the lesson of this storybook
Is: Don't judge folks by the way they look.

Don't judge them by their shape or size,
Or the color of their skin or eyes.

But treat others the way you want
them to treat you.
Don't ever forget that golden rule!

-THE END-

44065379R00022

Made in the USA
Charleston, SC
14 July 2015